This book belongs to ....

....

To read with ....

For Jonah, his book, from his great-godfather – M.M.

For David, Natasha & Luke, don't talk to pigeons – R.C.

RED SQUIRREL BOOKS

Published in 2014 in Great Britain by Barrington Stoke Ltd
18 Walker Street, Edinburgh, EH3 7LP

www.redsquirrelbooks.co.uk

This story was first published in a different form in *Wow! 366*, Scholastic Children's Books, 2008

Text © 2008 Michael Morpurgo
Illustrations © 2014 Ross Collins

A CIP catalogue record for this book is available from the British Library upon request

ISBN 978-1-78112-348-5

Printed in China by Toppan Leefung PTE. Ltd

All I Said Was

Michael Morpurgo
Ross Collins

RED SQUIRREL BOOKS

I looked up from my book, and saw a bird at my window.

All I said was, "Hi there, bird. You know what I'd like?

I'd like to be you. I'd like to be able to fly off to any place I liked. That would be so good."

And he said, "That's fine with me. Just open the window and I'll come in. I'll lie on your bed and read a book. I've always wanted to read a book."

So in he hopped, and off I flew.

I flew out over the roof-tops, and down towards the sea. I was thinking, 'Wings are the best, wings are great. This flying lark is amazing. I want to be a bird all my life.'

But then, as I skimmed low over the beach,
the gulls came after me. There was an
army of them, all out to get me.

So I flew in over the land,

over the rivers and fields. And what happened?

The crows mobbed me.

So I landed in a field to hide.

And what happened?

A farmer chased me.

I don't know how I got

out of there, but I did.

I had had enough of all this by now. I was thinking,
'Books are better, a whole lot better. Next time I'll
just read about being a bird.

I'll just imagine it. It'll be safer that way.
I'll live longer.' I flew back to town and landed
at my window.

And there he was, lying on my bed, reading my book. Only, the odd thing was, he didn't look like a bird any more.

He looked like me!

Then I saw myself in the window. I was still a bird!

I tapped on the window with my beak.

He looked up at me.

"Hi there, bird," he said. "You know what? I'm reading a great story. It's all about a boy like me who wants to be a bird like you. So he does a swap, and becomes a bird. Trouble is, it turns out he can't change back. He's a bird for the rest of his life. Isn't that a shame?"

Grow a love of reading

RED SQUIRREL BOOKS